AMICUS ILLUSTRATED • AMICUS INK

DO YOU REALLY WANT TO MEET
AN OWL?

WRITTEN BY BRIDGET HEOS   ILLUSTRATED BY DANIELE FABBRI

Amicus Illustrated and Amicus Ink
are imprints of Amicus
P.O. Box 1329
Mankato, MN 56002

Library of Congress Cataloging-in-Publication Data
Heos, Bridget, author.
Do you really want to meet an owl? / by Bridget
Heos ; illustrated by Daniele Fabbri.
    pages cm. — (Do you really want to meet...wild
animals?)
Audience: K to grade 3.
Summary: "After learning about several species
of an owl, a boy goes to the wilderness nearby to
observe owls' behavior in the wild"— Provided by
publisher.
ISBN 978-1-60753-948-3 (library binding) —
ISBN 978-1-68152-119-0 (pbk.) —
ISBN 978-1-68151-066-8 (ebook)
1. Owls—Behavior—Juvenile literature. 2. Owls—
Juvenile literature. I. Title.
QL696.S8H46 2016
598.9'7—dc23
                                                    2015034049

Editor: Rebecca Glaser
Designer : Kathleen Petelinsek

Printed in the United States of America at Corporate
Graphics in North Mankato, Minnesota.

HC 10 9 8 7 6 5 4 3 2 1
PB 10 9 8 7 6 5 4 3 2 1

ABOUT THE AUTHOR

Bridget Heos lives in Kansas City with her husband, four children, and an extremely dangerous cat . . . to mice, anyway. She has written more than 80 books for children, including many about animals. Find out more about her at www.authorbridgetheos.com.

ABOUT THE ILLUSTRATOR

Daniele Fabbri was born in Ravenna, Italy, in 1978. He graduated from Istituto Europeo di Design in Milan, Italy, and started his career as a cartoon animator, storyboarder, and background designer for animated series. He has worked as a freelance illustrator since 2003, collaborating with international publishers and advertising agencies.

Owls are interesting! But they are also fierce hunters. Are you sure you want to meet one in real life? Well, then you are in luck. Owls live on every continent except Antarctica.

An owl probably lives close to you! Do you live in the desert? You might see an elf owl nesting in a saguaro cactus. They are the smallest owls in the world—they are only the size of a pop can!

Perhaps you live in the arctic. Here, snowy owls' white feathers blend in with the snow. Snowy owls hunt during both day and night, but they are hard to spot!

Some owls, like the great horned owl, have a wide range. This owl lives in both North and South America. But owls are camouflaged. They blend in with nature. So you might hear the owl first. Listen! The great horned owl has a deep voice and says, "hoo hoo hoo."

Wait. That call sounds like a barred owl. It seems to ask a question. Wow! You might have two owls living near you. Let's see if we can spot one!

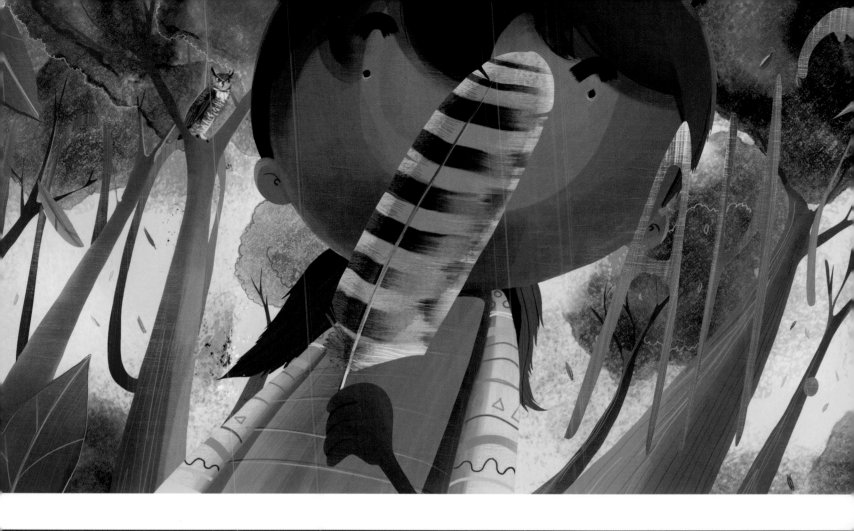

Here's a feather. It came from a great horned owl.
They hunt at dusk—when it's starting to get dark,
but there's still a little light. That's right now!

Shhh . . . owls hunt by listening.
The grass is rustling! Is it a mouse?
A rabbit? A small bird? Great
horned owls eat all these things.

Whoa! You didn't hear it coming, did you? With their big, feathery wings, owls fly silently.

The owl catches its prey with its talons. Pee-yoo! It's a skunk! The great horned owl is one of the only animals that will eat such a stinky critter!

13

Off it goes, carrying the heavy skunk.
Let's follow the owl to its nest.

Look! Baby owls. Careful! Owls are protective
parents. They will attack if you get too close.

And owls don't miss much. They can swivel their heads almost 270 degrees to see behind them. Their big pupils allow them to see at night. And owls have excellent hearing. An owl's real ears are hidden under feathers on each side of its face. Its "horns" look like ears, but they are just tufts of feathers.

Owls may be tough hunters, but they are kind parents. The mother owl keeps her babies warm. The father tears up the skunk with his beak and feeds it to the babies.

It's getting dark. Many owls are nocturnal. But you are not. Time to head back to your nest! And if you hear a strange hooting noise in the night, now you'll know "hoo" it is!

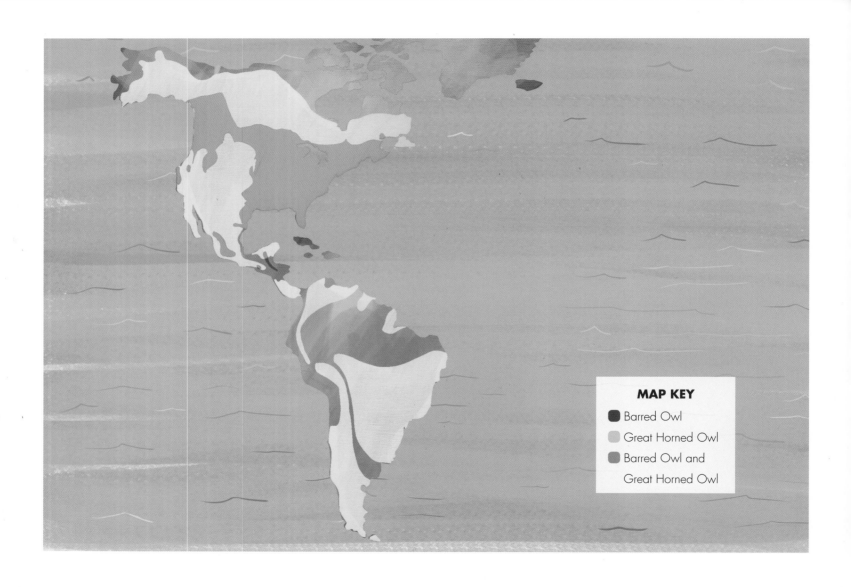

MAP KEY
- Barred Owl
- Great Horned Owl
- Barred Owl and Great Horned Owl

GLOSSARY

camouflaged Having colors and patterns that allow an animal to blend in to natural surroundings.

nocturnal Most active at night.

prey Animals that are hunted by another animal for food.

pupil The small, black, round area at the center of the eye.

swivel To turn or rotate around a central point.

talons The claws on a bird of prey.

READ MORE

Beaumont, Holly. *Why Do Owls and Other Birds Have Feathers?* Chicago: Heinemann Raintree, 2016.

Leaf, Christina. *Great Horned Owls*. Minneapolis: Bellwether Media, 2015.

Marsh, Laura. **Owls**. Washington, D.C.: National Geographic, 2014.

Phillips, Dee. **Burrowing Owl's Hideaway**. New York: Bearport Publishing, 2015.

WEBSITES

Journey North: Listen to Owls
http://www.learner.org/jnorth/tm/spring/OwlDictionary.html
Listen to all kinds of owl calls.

National Geographic Kids: Snowy Owl
http://kids.nationalgeographic.com/animals/snowy-owl/
Discover how fast the snowy owl can fly and its main source of food.

Owl Research Institute
http://www.owlinstitute.org/
See pictures of all kinds of owls, read more about their habitats, and listen to owl calls.

San Diego Zoo: Great Horned Owl
http://kids.sandiegozoo.org/animals/birds/great-horned-owl-1
Read about how the great horned owl got its name and look at close up pictures.

Every effort has been made to ensure that these websites are appropriate for children. However, because of the nature of the Internet, it is impossible to guarantee that these sites will remain active indefinitely or that their contents will not be altered.